Class No. _JC5 8)_ Acc No. _C/229278_

Author: _O'Brien, J_ Loc: _- 2 MAY 2008_

LEABHARLANN
CHONDAE AN CHABHAIN

1. **This book may be kept three weeks. It is to be returned on / before the last date stamped below.**
2. **A fine of 25c will be charged for every week or part of week a book is overdue.**

0 8 JAN 2009		
1 0 SEP 2009		
2 6 FEB 2011		
2 7 JAN 2012		

Dear Alfie

Happy Birthday. I'm sorry I can't be there...

Your loving Grandad

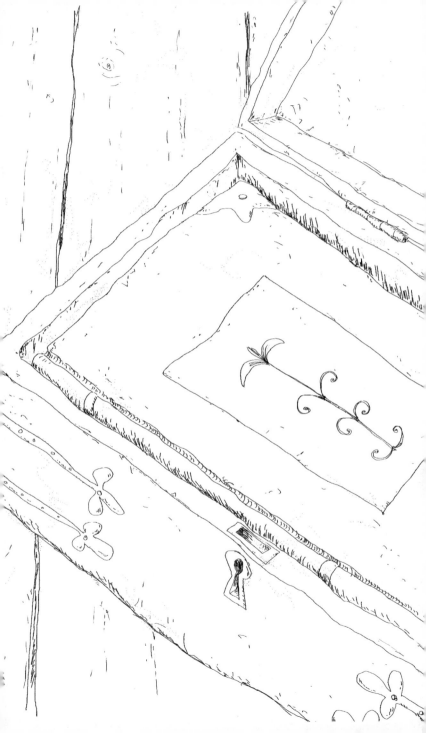

JOE O'BRIEN is an award-winning gardener who lives in Ballyfermot in Dublin. This is his first book about the wonderful world of Alfie Green.

DEDICATION

The *Alfie Green* series is dedicated to my son, Ethan, who in his short time in this world taught me to be strong, happy and thankful for the gift of life. Thank you, Ethan, for the inspiration to write.

ACKNOWLEDGEMENTS:

Thanks, firstly and especially, to Linda Kenny for your encouragement, your help in making this happen and your friendship.To Mary O'Sullivan, Patricia Crowley. To Mary Webb, Ide ní Laoghaire, Emma Byrne and all at O'Brien Press for their great work. Jean Texier for the wonderful illustrations. A special thanks to Michael O'Brien, the publisher.

To my late mum, who introduced me to the joys of gardening. My dad. My late and dear friend, Paddy Kelly. Finally, very special thanks to my wife and best friend Mandy.

*   *   *

JEAN TEXIER is a storyboard artist and illustrator. Initially trained in animation, he has worked in the film industry for many years.

Alfie Green

and the MAGICAL GIFT

Joe O'Brien

Illustrated by Jean Texier

THE O'BRIEN PRESS
DUBLIN

This paperback edition first published 2007 by The O'Brien Press Ltd.,
12 Terenure Road East, Rathgar, Dublin 6, Ireland.
Tel: +353 1 4923333; Fax: +353 1 4922777
E-mail: books@obrien.ie
Website: www.obrien.ie
Reprinted 2007.
First published 2005 in hardback by The O'Brien Press Ltd

ISBN: 978-1-84717-041-5

British Library Cataloguing-in-Publication Data
O'Brien, Joe
Alfie Green and the magical gift
1.Courage - Juvenile fiction 2.Magic - Juvenile fiction
3.Children's stories
I.Title II.Texier, Jean
823.9'2[J]

3 4 5 6 7 8 9 10
07 08 09 10 11

The O'Brien Press receives
assistance from

Editing, typesetting, layout, design: The O'Brien Press Ltd.
Illustrations: Jean Texier
Printed and bound in the UK by J.H. Haynes & Co Ltd, Sparkford

CONTENTS

CHAPTER 1

A Birthday Surprise

'From Grandad?' asked Alfie in surprise as he took the envelope from his granny.

'Yes, Alfie,' said his granny. 'Before your grandad died, he told me to give you this on your next birthday.'

Alfie shook the envelope. There was something heavy inside.

'Come and blow out your candles, Alfie,' his mother called from the livingroom.

Alfie slipped the envelope under
his T-shirt. 'I'll be back in a minute,'
he shouted as he ran through the
kitchen and out the back to his
grandad's shed.

Alfie locked the shed door behind him and ripped open the envelope.

Inside were a letter and a very old key.

He began to read.

Dear Alfie

Happy birthday. I'm sorry I can't be there, but I hope you will like my present.

There's a loose floorboard in the corner of the shed, behind my potting table. Lift it, and you'll find a box. Use the key to open the box.

Inside the box is an ancient book – a magical book. Open the book and you'll see a picture of a seed on the first page. Put your hand on the picture and all will be revealed.

Be brave, Alfie,

Your loving Grandad

Alfie put down the letter, his eyes bulging with excitement.

'Wow! A magical book!'

He moved the potting table and quickly found the loose floorboard. Underneath was a big, square box, covered in dust.

Alfie lifted it out and carried it to the table. He blew the dust off the lid and found the keyhole. With a little creak, the key turned in the lock and the box opened.

Alfie gazed at the magical book.
He was a little scared. Was it good
magic or bad magic?

There was only one way to find out. Taking a deep breath, he opened the book.

CHAPTER 2

MAGIC!

The first page was crinkled and yellow, and there, just as his grandad had said, was a picture of a seed.

Alfie's hand shook as he lowered it on to the picture.

The minute he touched the page

A BLINDING LIGHT

shot up into the air and threw him flat on his back on the floor.

Then the light faded and the picture of the seed transformed into a real seed.

It rose out of the book and began to spin.

As it did, it sprouted shoots, and out of the shoots came leaves.

Suddenly the spinning plant stopped.

It shook itself all over and a huge flower popped out from among the leaves.

'JEEPERS CREEPERS!'

Alfie gasped in amazement.

Alfie's grandad had grown hundreds of plants in his garden, but Alfie had never seen anything like this one.

Its stems were a maze of twists and turns and the leaves were large and crinkly and covered in pointy blue hairs.

But it was the flower that gave Alfie the biggest shock.

'You must be young Alfie Green,' said the flower.

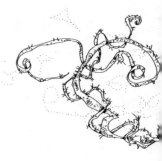

CHAPTER 3

DID YOU SAY SOMETHING?

Alfie was so astonished to hear the flower speak that he just stood there and stared, his mouth open so wide that you could have parked a bus in it.

'What?' he asked at last. 'What ... I mean ...who are you?'

'Oh! I'm just a wise old plant.'

Alfie had a hundred questions going around in his head.

His brain felt like the inside of his mother's washing machine on a

Saturday morning … spinning and spinning, non-stop.

Then the most important question

Jumped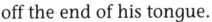

out of his head,

Hopped

into his mouth and

Rolled

off the end of his tongue.

'Wait a second! You can talk! How can you talk?'

The wise old plant laughed so hard that he shook all over and dropped one of his crinkly leaves.

It withered into a little mound of blue dust, which rose from the floor, glittering like millions of tiny stars, and settled on the pointy hairs of a new leaf.

The wise old planted smiled at Alfie.

'*All* plants can talk, Alfie. But only those with the gift can hear us.'

'Do I have the gift?' Alfie asked, and then felt silly. Of course he had the gift – wasn't he talking to a plant?

As if he could hear what Alfie was thinking, the wise old plant shook his head.

'Oh, it's not that simple,' he said. 'The gift has to be earned.'

'Your grandfather had the gift, Alfie, and you could have it too, but are you ready to earn it?'

'Yes, please,' said Alfie, and he really meant it.

CHAPTER 4

SIGN HERE!

The wise old plant turned over two pages of the magical book.

'Sign your name on this page, Alfie,' he said. He plucked one of his pointy blue hairs and handed it to Alfie. 'Use this.'

'How am I going to sign my name with a *hair*?' Alfie asked.

But when he looked down at his fingers, Alfie found he was holding a bright blue pen.

'Wow!' Alfie gasped, 'Magic! My granny would love to bring you to bingo with her. She's always losing her pens.'

Alfie signed his name in his best handwriting.

As soon as he had finished the last letter, his name began to disappear off the page.

Alfie Gree

'My name's gone!'

'Don't worry, Alfie. Your name has gone into the ancient book, and is now written on the crystal orchid that is waiting for you in my world.'

'Orchid? *Your* world?' Alfie was very confused.

'Yes,' the plant explained. 'The crystal orchid is the shining light that connects the world of talking plants – my world, to this world – your world. The power of the orchid allows its keeper to hear what the plants are saying.'

He pointed to a biscuit box on a shelf near the door of the shed.

'That's where your grandfather kept his orchid.'

Alfie took down the box and lifted out a glass flower. It looked very ordinary.

'But it's not shining,' he said to the plant.

For a moment the wise old plant looked sad. 'Yes, its light faded when your grandfather signed his name on the last page of the ancient book.'

'Why?'

'Because he was going to die and it was time to sign the last page and pass the gift on to you, Alfie.'

Now it was Alfie's turn to be sad.

The wise old plant lifted up Alfie's chin with his crinkly leaf and wiped the tear from his eye.

'So, do you still want to accept your grandfather's gift?'

'More than anything,' replied Alfie.

'Then this is what you must do.
First, you must return your
grandfather's orchid to the shining
orchid plant at the top of the
crooked tree.

'There you will find a crystal orchid with your name on it. Once you've got this, Alfie, you will be returned to this world. Then, and only then will you have the gift.'

'But how do I get to your world?' Alfie asked. 'And how do I find the crooked tree?'

'Go out through the shed door,' instructed the wise old plant. 'There you will find friends to guide you. They know the way. But remember this, Alfie: not all things in my world are friendly.'

With that, the wise old plant folded itself back into the book, which closed with a

CHAPTER 5

ARCANIA

Alfie opened the shed door and stepped outside.

'Hey! Where's the garden gone?' He looked around in amazement.

'This isn't my back garden. This must
be the wise old plant's world.'

'You can say that again! Welcome to Arcania,' said a voice behind him.

'Who said that?' Alfie yelled.

'Me,' said a spade, as he leapt out of the soil.

Alfie couldn't believe his eyes. First, talking plants and now a talking spade. What next?

'I'm Alfie Green,' he said to the spade.

'Pleased to meet you, Alfie Green,' the spade replied. 'I'm Paddy the spade O'Toole.'

Alfie burst out laughing.

'What's so funny?' asked the spade.

'Sorry!' laughed Alfie. 'I've never heard of a spade called Paddy. Where did you get your name?'

'From your grandad. He had so much trouble with my real name that he suggested a name he could remember.'

'We were all sad when we heard that the light of his crystal orchid had faded,' Paddy added.

'We?' asked Alfie.

'How rude of me!' said the spade. 'Come on out, lads.'

Out from behind the shed appeared a fork, clippers and a hoe.

Paddy introduced them:

'Alfie Green, meet

Vinny the fork,

Mick the hoe,

and Jimmy the clippers.'

Paddy, Vinny, Mick and Jimmy – Grandad had named the garden tools after his pals from the darts club!

Alfie told his new friends about his quest to find the crooked tree, and they agreed to take him there.

CHAPTER 6

SLEEPY MEADOWS

Jimmy the clippers opened his blades and began to walk ahead, followed by Alfie, with Paddy the spade, Vinny the fork and Mick the hoe hopping along beside them.

After walking for two hours, Alfie's feet were killing him.

'Are we there yet?' he asked.

'Not too far now,' said Paddy. 'There's a swamp up ahead – a nasty place. We'll have to go through that to reach the crooked tree, but first we must cross Sleepy Meadows.'

'Sleepy Meadows?' Alfie asked.

'Just over there, Alfie,'
Jimmy pointed with one of his blades and nearly fell
over.

Alfie ran
ahead of the
others.

'Wow, MASSIVE!' he called back as he saw field after field packed with blue lavender.

'It looks like Croke Park when the Dubs are playing.'

'Croke Park? Dubs?' Vinny the fork looked at Paddy the spade, who shook his head.

'Football,' Alfie explained. 'Haven't you ever played football?'

'Oh, that thing with the roundy ball?' Paddy remembered.

'Your grandad tried to teach us, but Vinny and Jimmy kept puncturing the ball, so he gave up.'

Suddenly Alfie heard a familiar sound. Someone was sNORing!

ZZZzz..
ZZZzz..
ZZZzz..

'It's the lavenders. All they ever do is sleep and snore,' explained Mick the hoe. 'That's why it's called Sleepy Meadows.'

As the five friends brushed their way through the sleeping lavenders, the noise grew louder and louder.

'I'll never complain about my brother's snoring again,' Alfie yawned.

Then Vinny yawned.

Then Mick yawned.

'Uh-oh!' said Paddy the spade.

'Eh! What?' asked Alfie.

'I forgot to tell you that if the lavenders snore very loudly, they breathe out a sleeping dust that can make you very drowsy.'

Alfie laughed. 'Is that all? You had me worried there, Paddy.'

'No, that's not all. You don't want
to be drowsy walking through Sleepy
Meadows. You need to be on the
lookout for–'

'**OW!**' interrupted Alfie. 'Something
bit me on the bum!'

'–**SNAPPING DRAGONS**!' yelled Paddy the spade. 'You need to be on the lookout for Snapping Dragons. Run for it!'

Alfie legged it through the meadows, followed by the tools.

'Ow! My ankle!'

Alfie had been bitten again. The Snapping Dragons seemed to like the taste of boy.

Vinny the fork felt sorry for Alfie. 'Quick, Alfie. Hang on to my handle.'

Alfie grabbed hold of the handle and Vinny began to spring up into the air like a pogo stick.

Every time his prongs dug into the soil, it became annoyed and pushed him back out again.

Vinny sprang Alfie right out of Sleepy Meadows and away from the bum-biting, ankle-grabbing Snapping Dragons.

Soon Paddy and Mick had joined them. Jimmy the clippers was last, but he didn't mind the Snapping Dragons; he just cut their heads off whenever they attacked him.

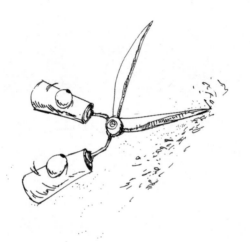

CHAPTER 7

THE EVIL SWAMP

'We must keep going,' Paddy told Alfie, who was feeling very sorry for himself. 'Look, there's the swamp.'

'Phew, what a pong!' Alfie held his nose as the evil smell reached him. 'How are we going to get across?'

There was a strange-looking boat near the banks, but it had no oars.

'Now what?' Alfie asked. 'We have to have something to push our way through that mess.'

'Use me,' volunteered Mick the hoe. 'Good idea,' agreed Alfie, and he grabbed Mick and pushed off from the bank.

The swamp was very cold, and dark, and scary.

Every now and
then a strange
whistling noise
blew around the
boat, and then
faded back into
the mist.

Pops and groans and sucking noises came from the swamp.

'I don't like this at all,' Alfie whispered, and he stopped paddling until Mick the hoe bubbled at him to

take his head out of the water.

As Alfie raised his arm to begin paddling again, something slimy hit him on his cheek.

'**YEEUCK!**' What was that?'

'Keep your head down, Alfie,' shouted Paddy the spade.

He leaned forward and shielded
Alfie's face with his flat metal head.

'It's the Venom-Spitting Lilies. If
they get you in the eye you're in real
trouble.'

Alfie could hear the spits going *Ping, Ping* off Paddy's head. He paddled like mad until Paddy gave him the all-clear that they were safely away from the horrid plants.

CHAPTER 8

GUARDIANS OF THE CROOKED TREE

Everything was quiet for a while. Then Jimmy, who had been keeping lookout at the front of the boat, called out, 'The crooked tree!'

Up ahead, an old, crooked tree leaned against a crumbling wall.

Alfie and the tools hauled the boat onto the bank and walked towards the tree.

'Uh-oh!' said Paddy suddenly. 'The Guardians!'

Alfie hated when Paddy said
'Uh-oh!' It always meant trouble. And
trouble was just what was waiting for
them.

Six Giant Hogweeds had formed a
circle around the foot of the crooked
tree and were stamping their roots
in and out of the ground.

'Can they hurt?' asked Alfie nervously.

'Can they WHAT?' replied Paddy. 'Forget about Snapping Dragons and Spitting Lilies; one swipe from these guys and you'll break out in agonising blisters.'

Alfie shivered. For a minute he thought about giving up altogether. Then an absolutely brilliant idea *sprang* into his head.

'Vinny,' he asked. 'Could you do your pogo-ing trick again, and spring me over the Hogweeds, onto the wall?'

'I could try.'

Alfie grabbed hold of Vinny's handle and wrapped his legs around the shaft.

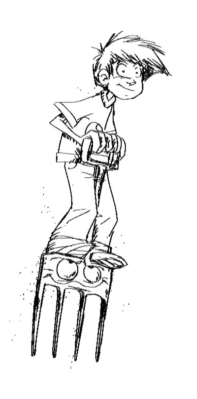

Vinny did a few practice springs, getting higher and higher each time. Then, with one mighty push he sprang right over the heads of the Giant Hogweeds and, just at the last minute, Alfie let go and jumped for the wall.

All the tools cheered as Alfie dragged himself up on the wall and edged his way along to the tree.

He started to climb from one crooked branch to the next, until at last he saw something bright just above him – the shining orchid plant!

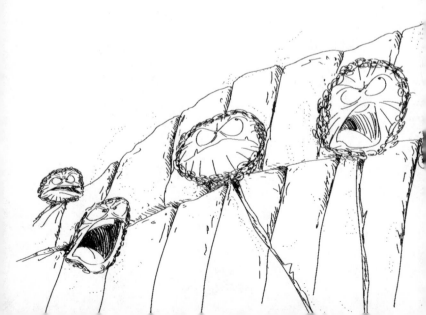

Then Alfie's foot slipped.

He grabbed hold of the ivy that
wound around the tree and managed
to stop himself falling.

CHAPTER 9

CAUGHT!

'Uh-oh!' said Paddy the spade. 'I forgot to tell him about the crying ivy.'

Alfie didn't hear Paddy because just then all the babies in the entire world started screaming in his ears.

At least, that's what it sounded like to poor Alfie.

Waaaaaaagh!

Waaaaaaaaaaaaaaaaaaaaaaaaaaagh!

The crying ivy wrapped itself around his legs and began pulling him down. Alfie hung on until he couldn't stand the noise any longer.

He took his hands off the tree and stuck his fingers in his ears. The ivy was up to his waist now.

Suddenly the crying stopped.

Alfie heard 'Snip, Snip, Snip'. He looked down and saw Jimmy the clippers cutting his way through the ivy at the bottom of the tree.

Soon Alfie's legs were free as the ivy turned and ran down to attack Jimmy.

'Quick, Alfie. Climb faster,' yelled Jimmy.

At last Alfie reached the shining orchid plant. He took his grandad's orchid out of his pocket. He placed the glass flower into the plant and it instantly lit up.

Then it dimmed and a new flower
shone in its place – a glowing crystal
orchid with the name **Alfie Green**
written on it!

Wow! His very own crystal orchid.

Feeling just a teeny bit scared, Alfie reached out for his orchid and grasped it around the stem.

CHAPTER 10

GOODBYE TO ARCANIA

A white light

SHOT OUT

of the orchid, and for a moment
Alfie could see nothing.

When his eyes cleared, Alfie was no longer up the crooked tree in Arcania.

He was in his grandad's shed, back home.

Alfie gazed at his shining crystal orchid for a while, and then put it into the biscuit tin.

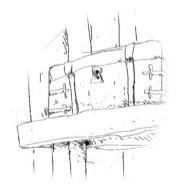

He hid the box with the ancient book and the key under the floorboard.

He locked the shed door behind him and walked out into the garden.

All the plants in Alfie's garden were cheeering – and Alfie could hear them, every single one of them.

HE HAD THE GIFT

Suddenly Alfie thought, 'How long have I been away? Is it still my birthday?'

He heard a shout from the kitchen. 'Alfieeeeeeeee! Your candles are nearly out.' It was his mother.

'Wow!' Said Alfie. ' Time hasn't moved at all.'

He ran in to blow out his candles and celebrate the best birthday ever, as Alfie Green, Keeper of the Crystal Orchid.

And now that he had the connection between his world and Arcania, he knew that someday he would go back to see his friends Paddy and Jimmy and Vinny and Mick.

READ ALFIE'S OTHER GREAT ADVENTURES IN:

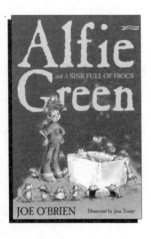

Alfie Green and a Sink Full of Frogs

Hundreds of tiny eyes peep up at Alfie Green from the sink in his garden. Frogs! Who invited them? And when the frogs tell their friends and relations about their great new swimming pool, the place is invaded. Alfie needs help — fast.

This is a job for the magic book that Alfie has inherited from his grandad. And the magic book comes up with a very unusual way of solving Alfie's problem.

Alfie Green and the Bee-Bottle Gang

Alfie is in big trouble.

He stopped Whacker Walsh and his gang from trapping bees in the park and now they are out to get him. What can he do?

The wise old plant in the magical book comes up with a plan that sends Alfie back to Arcania in search of the Queen Bee in Honeycomb Mountain.

Alfie needs back-up — and he needs it NOW!

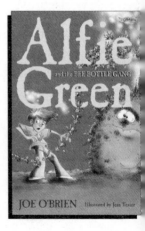

Alfie Green and the Fly-Trapper

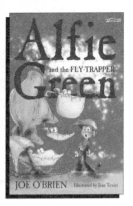

Alfie's house is invaded by flies. His fly-trap plant is too small to eat them all so the wise old plant uses magic to make it bigger.

Then it gets BIGGER and BIGGER and BIGGER. Nothing is safe! Alfie decides the only place for the Giant Fly Trapper is in the Belching Bogs in Arcania.

But to get there he must outwit the creatures of the Nanabur Mines and the deadly worm monster.

Alfie Green and the Monkey Puzzler

The circus has come to town. But it's no ordinary circus, it's Monty's Marvellous Monkey Circus and all the performers are monkeys!

All the kids from Budsville are really excited, except for Alfie who suspects all is not what it seems ...

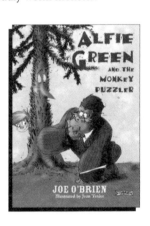

Alfie Green and the Conker King

Alfie would love to win the School Conker Championship. But with Conor Hoolihan on his team and Whacker Walsh cheating all the time, he has no chance. He needs to find a Super Cracking Conker, and he needs to find one fast.

Alfie must travel through the Skeleton Woods of Arcania to find the last great king of the conker warriors.

Will the Conker King part with his winning conker?

CHECK OUT ALL OUR CHILDREN'S BOOKS ON

www.obrien.ie

The Swamp

The C...

Sleepy Meadows

Alfie's House

BUDSVILLE AVENU

The
Wonderful World of
Alfie Green

SYCAMORE ROAD

LAUREL PARK

BUDSVILLE
PRIMARY
SCHOOL